"Home is where the heart is,
home is where the fart is.
Come let us fart in the home.
There is no art in a fart.
Still a fart may not be artless.
Let us fart and artless fart in
the home."

-Ernest Hemingway

A is for Antelope

Antelope mostly live in vast grasslands,
and their farts sound like out of tune brass bands!

F is for FART

By: MR. Smelt It & MRS. Dealt It

B is for Badger

Honey badgers - so fierce it's not **funny**;
bees hide from their farts and lose their **honey**!

C is for Camel

Some camels have one hump, and some have two,
but all camels have farts that smell like poo!

D is for Dinosaur

"Dinosaur" means terrifying lizard;
their farts were like a repulsive blizzard!

E is for Elephant

Elephants are smart, large, and so **wondrous**; when they let one rip it's quite **thunderous!**

F is for Ferret

Ferrets dance when they are feeling **afraid**,
and when they toot your nose will feel **dismayed!**

G is for Giraffe

Giraffes can stand up to twenty feet **tall**;
their farts smell like rotting leaves in the **fall!**

H is for Hare

A male hare is a jack, a female jill;
when they pass gas, you'll tumble down the hill!

I is for Iguana

Iguanas fart, and it's pretty **funny**;
it's funny unless the farts turn **runny**!

J is for Jaguar

Jaguars hunt while being very **stealthy**,
but their toots stink more than what seems **healthy!**

K is for Kangaroo

Kangaroos live in groups called mobs, you see,
and when they pass gas, they do it with glee!

L is for Lemur

The name "lemur" means spirits of the night; they take delight in having a stink fight!

M is for Manatee

A manatee is an aquatic **beast,**
whose farts smell appalling, to say the **least!**

N is for Narwhal

Narwhals are unicorns of the **ocean**;
their butts make a noxious bubble **potion**!

O is for Otter

Otters are playful and stay up all **night**;
their farts smell like fish – it isn't **alright!**

P is for Pelican

Pelicans can't fart, their butts are a **bore**,
but they drop poop down below as they **soar**!

Q is for Qinling Panda

Qinling pandas eat bamboo for their snacks,
but watch out when their flatulence attacks!

R is for Rhino

Rhinos farts will knock you right off your **feet**;
the stench of their toots really can't be **beat!**

S is for Sloth

Sloths - they hang around taking life **easy**;
they're too cool to have a butt that's **breezy**!

T is for Turtle

Turtles make great ninjas, we all know **that**;
just keep your distance when their butts go **splat**!

U is for Unicorn

Unicorns have rocket blasters, you know;
they blast great big farts and away they go!

V is for Vervet Monkey

Vervet monkeys play all day and all **night**; having fun and farting to their **delight!**

W is for Whale

The scale of this whale is rather **immense**;
your nose will surely know to take **offense!**

X is for X-Ray Tetra

Most fish don't fart, x-ray fish **included**;
they don't have to wonder which friend **tooted**!

Y is for Yak

Yaks wander at a high **elevation**;
their farts smell like a stinky gas **station**!

Z is for Zebra

Zebras pass gas when you give them a fright;
that's a real stinky take on fight or flight!

Also available

Make learning **fun** with this **hilarious** activity book!

G is for Giraffe

Giraffes can stand up to twenty feet **tall**; their farts smell like rotting leaves in the **fall**!

F is for FART

Handwriting Activity Book

Made in the USA
Columbia, SC
24 March 2020